Mcr
MCR

EVANSTON PUBLIC LIBRARY
W9-BHR-913

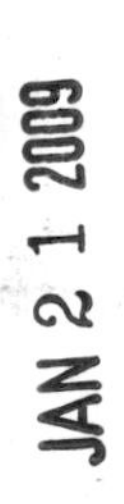
JAN 2 1 2009

WALKER & COMPANY
NEW YORK

With love and thanks to Diana

First published in the United States of America in 2008 by Walker Publishing Company, Inc.
Distributed to the trade by Macmillan

For information about permission to reproduce selections from this book, write to
Permissions, Walker & Company, 175 Fifth Avenue, New York, New York 10010

Library of Congress Cataloging-in-Publication Data
Richards, Chuck.
Critter sitter / Chuck Richards.
p. cm.
Summary: When the Mahoney family hires Henry the Critter Sitter to watch their dog, cat, bird, fish, frog, and snake, he thinks he is up for the challenge since creature control is his game, but the pets have a different idea.
ISBN-13: 978-0-8027-9595-3 • ISBN-10: 0-8027-9595-1 (hardcover)
ISBN-13: 978-0-8027-9596-0 • ISBN-10: 0-8027-9596-X (reinforced)
[1. Pets—Fiction. 2. Pet sitting—Fiction. 3. Humorous stories.] I. Title.
PZ7.R37858Cr 2008 [E]—dc22 2008004314

Typeset in Colwell
Art created with colored pencil and watercolor on paper
Book design by Daniel Roode

Visit Walker & Company's Web site at www.walkeryoungreaders.com

Printed in China
2 4 6 8 10 9 7 5 3 1 (hardcover)
2 4 6 8 10 9 7 5 3 1 (reinforced)

"Your Critter Sitter, reporting for duty!" announced Henry to Mr. and Mrs. Mahoney, his very first customers. They were picking up their kids from Camp Yippie-Yahoo.

"Now, Henry," warned Mr. Mahoney, "our snake is an escape artist, so keep that dumbbell on top of his tank."

"Don't you worry about a thing," assured Henry. "Critter Sitter is my name and Creature Control is my game."

Slobberchops wasn't the brainiest beast on the planet, but he immediately befriended Henry. Little Miss Purr-fect considered

herself the queen of cats and had no need for babysitters. The boa constrictor just flicked his forky tongue at Henry from behind the glass.

That evening, the dog took the Critter Sitter for a run around the block, whizzing past the gloomy mansion at the top of the hill. Mrs. Angora lived alone in the creepy house, and all the neighborhood kids thought she was very weird.

When they got home from their walk, Henry closed Slobberchops in the laundry room and then made sure all the other animals were settled in for the night.

"SEE YOU LATER, ALLIGATOR," screeched Peepers, the cockatiel, as Henry left for home.

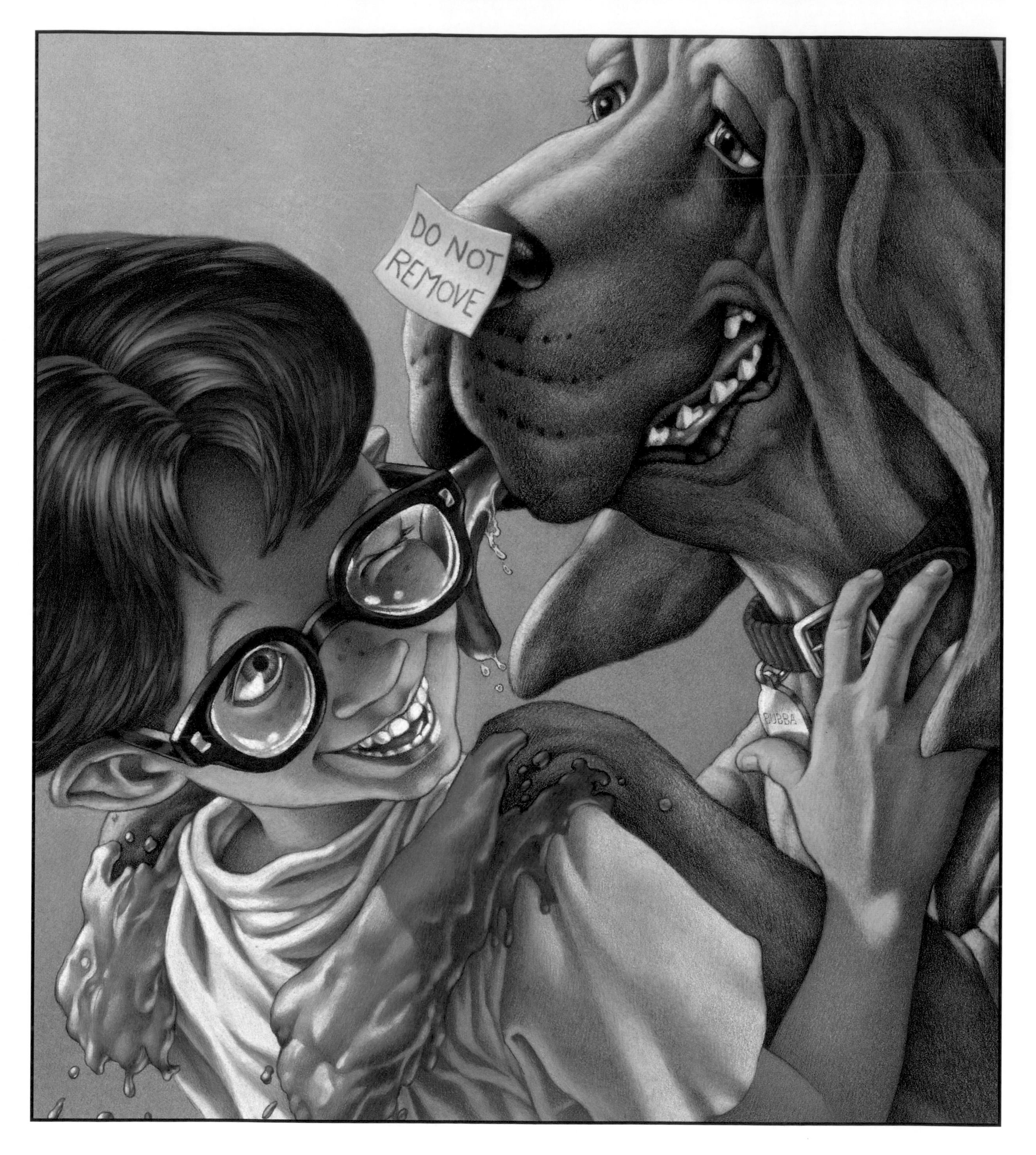

Early the next morning, the Critter Sitter was greeted by two goopy blue paws flopping onto his shoulders.

"Ewww! Get off me, ya big doofus! How did you get out of the laundry room, anyway?"

Henry followed the blue dog tracks leading into the dining room.

"Holy smokes!"

The snake's aquarium was open . . . and empty. All clues pointed to Slobberchops as the culprit.

A queasy feeling flooded over Henry. Would a snake eat a cat . . . or a dog . . . or a KID?

Henry immediately checked the sinks, bathtub, and toilet. Then he followed the slimy trail into the laundry room. It was a disaster area. Henry dragged the dog out to the garage so he could clean up the mess.

An hour later, Henry was ready to give the dog a bath. Little Miss Purr-fect yowled as Slobberchops SHOOK-SHOOK-SHOOK, spraying sheets of soapy water everywhere. The wet Critter Sitter was relieved to see that she hadn't become a snake snack.

Breakfast was late, so Henry opened a can of Kitty Delight. Next, he cracked open a box of crickets to feed Flip, the tree frog. While he lifted the tank lid, the cat knocked the cricket box off the counter.

"Oh, that's just great!" cried Henry.

Suddenly Flip escaped through the open lid as Slobberchops jumped up and unlatched the door, barreling down the block in hot pursuit of a bunny he saw grazing in the yard.

The dog chased the rabbit up the hill and through Mrs. Angora's iron gate. No kid had ever dared to step foot on this property before.

Henry raced around a hedge and stopped dead—it was a rabbit's paradise!
"**ROO-ROO-ROOF**," barked Slobberchops, and rabbits scattered.

Soon the pooch's front paws were digging holes so fast they were a blur. Henry was fumbling to clip the leash to the dog's collar when Mrs. Angora appeared . . . with a pair of sharp, shimmering shears!

"W-w-we were j-j-just leaving!" he stammered as he somersaulted backward over the bloodhound. "The f-f-frog and the snake have both escaped!" His fear gave him the strength to drag the dog away.

"What a very, very strange little boy," Mrs. Angora said to herself.

Back at the house, Henry stumbled back to the tub with the muddy mutt. Little Miss Purr-fect yowled as Slobberchops SHOOK-SHOOK-SHOOK, spraying sheets of soapy water everywhere.

"That's it," scolded Henry. "You're grounded, buddy boy." And he marched the dog back to the garage.

The kitchen was crawling with crickets. Henry got down on his hands and knees to track down the snake and the frog when he noticed something move overhead.

S-S-Slinky was hanging from a curtain rod over the bird's now-empty cage!

Henry's head spun as he imagined a nightmarish vision.

The notorious Critter Sitter was on trial. His crime: animal neglect in the first degree. Prosecutor Purr-fect's hissing cross-examination convinced everyone of his guilt. A jury of crickets chanted, "EXTERMINATE—EXTERMINATE—EXTERMINATE—EXTERMINATE . . ."

Judge Slobberchops sentenced Henry to the maximum sentence: 525 dog years in prison, without parole.

Suddenly the convicted "jailbird" was being tormented by a feathered prison guard that **PECK-PECK-PECKED** at the cage with its sharp, shiny beak.

Henry was jolted back to reality by an earsplitting **CRASH** and **CLATTER** in the garage, where he found the bucket-headed bloodhound.

Henry lugged the smelly beast down the hall and into the tub. Little Miss Purr-fect yowled as Slobberchops SHOOK-SHOOK-SHOOK, spraying sheets of soapy water everywhere.

Just then, Henry heard a familiar squawk.

"PRET-TY BIRD! PRET-TY, PRET-TY BIRD!" A freaky, feather-tailed puppet waddled down the hall. A spooked Slobberchops knocked over the fishbowl, hurling Bubbles, the goldfish, through the air in a spectacular swan dive.

Little Miss Purr-fect prepared to pounce, but the Critter Sitter leaped over her, heroically snatched up the fish, and put her into the shiny white toilet bowl.

Henry went through the house, swabbing all the floors clean. He had just refilled the fishbowl when he heard the toilet start to flush!

Henry bolted into the bathroom, plunged his hand into the bowl, and saved Bubbles from being sucked down into a gurgling grave.

Henry scowled and hissed at the cat culprit through clenched teeth. "You're a Little Miss Pain-in-the-Neck!"

"SEE YOU LATER, ALLIGATOR!"

Henry returned to the kitchen just in time to watch S-S-Slinky disappearing down the drain.

Henry grabbed hold of the snake—and tugged and tugged with all his might. Finally the reptile surrendered and was pulled free.

Exhausted, Henry and S-S-Slinky collapsed on the floor. A cricket suddenly landed on Henry's nose, and Flip flopped over to finish his feast.

Henry slowly reached into the cabinet and quietly grabbed a shiny spaghetti strainer. Taking aim, he clanked the cookware down onto his head, then carefully reached under and captured the tree frog.

Henry heard a car turning into the driveway. The Mahoneys were back. Peepers hopped across the counter and onto the dining-room table.

"Great!" Henry moaned. "I'll never catch that pesky bird!" He unwound the snake from his neck, put him in his tank, and put the dumbbell back on top just as the front door opened.

Becky and Bobby Mahoney ran inside as Slobberchops charged toward the door. There was so much commotion that only Henry heard Peepers squawk, "SEE YOU LATER, ALLIGATOR!" The bird swooped back into the open cage and closed its door with her hooked beak as everyone spilled into the kitchen.

Mrs. Mahoney looked around and smiled as she opened her purse. "You've done a fine job, Henry. It sure seems like you've kept everything under control here."

"Um, well, ah . . . Creature Control *is* my game," replied Henry sheepishly.

The Mahoneys rewarded the Critter Sitter with a hefty bonus. "Oh, and Henry," Mrs. M. said, "we'll be taking a three-week vacation in August. You simply must do this again for us, won't you, dear?"

The Critter Sitter's eyes nearly popped out of his head. He was truly *PET*-RIFIED!

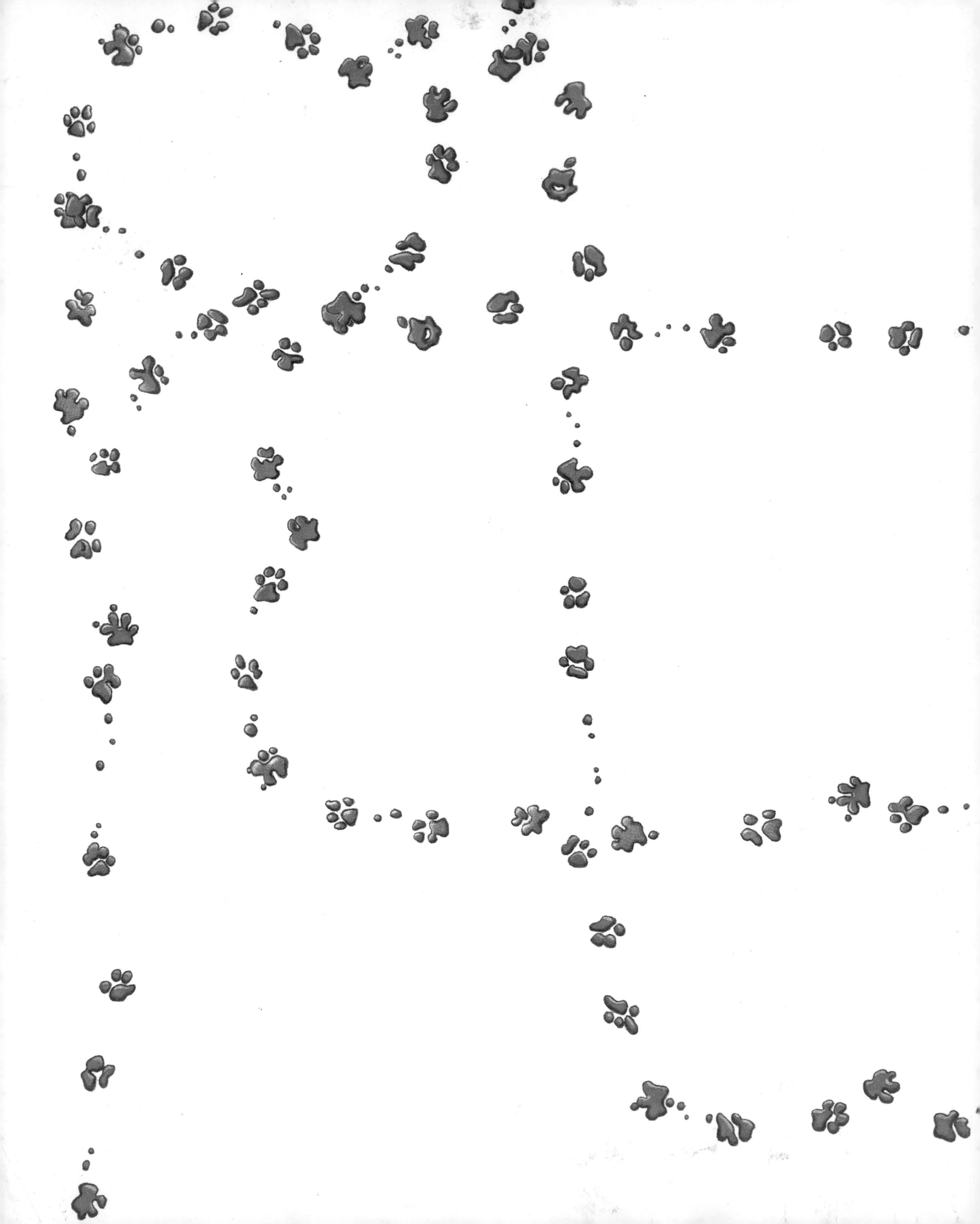